A NOTE TO PARENTS

Early Step into Reading Books are designed for preschoolers and kindergartners who are just getting ready to read. The words are easy, the type is big, and the stories are packed with rhyme, rhythm, and repetition.

We suggest that you read this book to your child the first few times, pointing to each word as you go. Soon your child will start saying the words with you. And before long, he or she will try to read the story alone. Don't be surprised if your child uses the pictures to figure out the text—that's what they're there for! The important thing is to develop your child's confidence—and to show your child that reading is fun.

When your child is ready to move on, try the rest of the steps in our Step into Reading series. **Step 1 Books** (preschool–grade 1) feature the same easy-to-read type as the Early Step into Reading Books, but with more words per page. **Step 2 Books** (grades 1–3) are both longer and slightly more difficult, while **Step 3 Books** (grades 2–3) introduce readers to paragraphs and fully developed plot lines. **Step 4 Books** (grades 2–4) offer exciting nonfiction for the increasingly independent reader.

The grade levels assigned to the five steps are intended only as guides. Some children move through all five steps very rapidly; others climb the steps over a period of several years. Either way, these books will help your child "step into reading" in style!

www.randomhouse.com/kids
Visit Theodore Tugboat on the Internet at
www.cochran.com/theodore or www.pbs.org/tugboat.

Library of Congress Cataloging-in-Publication Data
Man-Kong, Mary. Theodore and the scary cove / by Mary Man-Kong ; illustrated by Cardona Studios.
p.   cm. — (Early step into reading)
SUMMARY: Two tugboats decide to go to a cove where, in the dark, everything looks spooky and frightening.
ISBN: 0-375-80508-7 (pbk.) — ISBN: 0-375-90508-1 (lib. bdg.) [1. Tugboats—Fiction. 2. Night—Fiction.] I. Cardona, Jose Marie, ill. II. Title. III. Series. PZ7.M31215Tg 2000 [E]—dc21 99-35231

Printed in the United States of America July 2000 10 9 8 7 6 5 4 3 2 1

1578539

Early Step into Reading™

Theodore
and the
Scary Cove

by Mary Man-Kong
illustrated by Cardona Studios

From the *Theodore Tugboat* television series created by Andrew Cochran

Random House 🏠 New York

"Let's go to the cove,"
says Hank.

The tugboats chug
along the water.

It is night.

The cove is dark.

Theodore sees a
scary shape.

Is it a monster?

The scary shape makes
a scary sound.

Creeek-o! Creeek-o!

"It <u>is</u> a monster!" says Theodore. He and Hank race back home!

It is a new day.

The sun is shining.

Today, Theodore has
to work at the cove.

Theodore is scared.
What if he sees the
monster?

Theodore sees a shape.
But today it does not
look scary.

It is a tree!

Creeek-o! Creeek-o!

What is that sound?

Theodore sees
a small frog.

"Are you the monster?"
Theodore asks.

"*Creeek-o! Creeek-o!*"

says the frog.

Theodore laughs.

The cove is not a scary

place after all!